A Tall Tale

by Lizz Meredith

Illustrations by: Lizz Meredith
Book design by: SWATT Books Ltd

Printed in the United Kingdom
First Printing, 2021

ISBN: 978-1-9196359-0-3 (Paperback)

Lizz Meredith
Stockport, Greater Manchester
maryjolisamcduff@googlemail.com

It's bedtime and the shadow on the wall is back.

A shadow on the wall. What is it? Is it a giraffe?

But it cannot be as a giraffe lives in Africa, and not in **my** bedroom.

A shadow on the
wall. What is it?
Is it a dinosaur?

But it cannot be
as dinosaurs are
extinct, and not
in **my** bedroom.

A shadow on the wall. What is it? Is it an octopus tentacle?

But it cannot be as an octopus lives under the sea, and not in **my** bedroom.

A shadow on the wall. What is it? Is it a swan?

But it cannot be as a swan lives at a lake, and not in **my** bedroom.

A shadow on the
wall. What is it?
Is it a peacock
feather?

But it cannot be
as a peacock lives
in India, and not
in **my** bedroom.

A shadow on the
wall. What is it?
Is it a periscope?

But it cannot be as
periscopes are found
in submarines, and
not in **my** bedroom.

A shadow on the wall. What is it? Is it an ostrich?

But it cannot be as an ostrich lives in the hot dessert, and not in **my** bedroom.

The shadow
on the wall.
Where has it gone?

Hello Dave!
Ha Ha - it was my
cat's tail all the time!

He lives in my
bedroom.

Night, Night Dave!

Sleep tight.

And don't let the
bed bugs bite!

Don't be afraid
of the dark.

The dark lets you
see the universe we
all live in. You can
see the beautiful
moon, and the
stars from your
bedroom window!

The End

Hello
It's me Dave!
Hope you enjoyed
the tale of my
'Tall' tail.
It's going to
be a beautiful
night, tonight.
See you later!
x x

This book is dedicated to
Miss Mallam

Lightning Source UK Ltd.
Milton Keynes UK
UKRC011915170821
388941UK00003B/1